FOOTPRINTS
OF
A GUNFIGHTER

SAM TURLEY

Sam Turley had only been asleep for a short time in a foul-smelling hotel room. Sounds of gunfire brought him out of bed. Not fully awake yet, but his instinct had already kicked-in, he grabbed the Colt from his holster.

Slowly edging toward the hotel window, he looked down into the dusty street. Rubbing his eyes to see better, he saw two men sharing a bottle of whiskey. The taller of the two was firing his pistol in the air.

Suddenly, the sheriff and his two deputies, with shotguns, approached the men. Ordering them to drop their weapons. The taller of the men wasn't moving fast enough for one deputy. He banged him hard across the head with his shot-gun, knocking him to the ground.

Ordering the other man to pick him up as they escorted the two men off to jail. The sheriff, a rather large man in his late forties with a handle-bar mustache had paid Sam a visit earlier that morning just after he checked-in the hotel. He came to room with his two deputies to order him out of town.

Informing Sam, "we don't need a gunfighter with your reputation in our town."

Sam informed the sheriff he had affairs to take care of with his lawyer. Soon as his business was done, he would gladly leave town. If that was not fast enough for him. He better talk with Sam's lawyer, also, the mayor of the town. Because he's the one who sent it to him. After pondering the day's events, Sam returns to the bed with the lumpy mattress. A warm breeze blew into the open hotel window. Smelling the stables across the street. He was plum tuckered out from the long journey.

It was hotter than a whorehouse on a nickel night.

He lay in bed trying to get back to sleep. Finally dozing off around midnight to the quiet of the night.

Sun-light was already in the room when Sam woke-up, drenched in sweat. He staggered over to the dresser where a vase of water was. He began pouring some into a bowl to wash his face. Grabbing a towel, he wiped the water from his eyes.

Glancing into the mirror, he noticed an elderly gray-haired, wrinkled face staring back at him. Thinking *'where has all the time gone.'* He had his fair share of misery and pain. Lived most of his life by the gun. Something he wasn't proud of, but the gun became a necessary tool in his life. The people he knew and cared about the most were all gone. This younger generation didn't care about an old man and his memories. He finished combing his gray hair. Grabbed his broad-brimmed black Stetson hat and put on his pearl-handled guns. He walked toward the door to go downstairs to the hotel cafe. When someone knocked on his door. Opening it, he encountered a very nervous young man.

A slightly built man clutching a derby hat in his hands. Wearing a checkered suit and bow tie.

Sam told the young man he was just leaving for dinner. Whatever he was selling, he wasn't interested in buying.

The young man introduced himself as Robert Gray, a reporter for the New York Sun. It would be his honor to buy Sam's dinner, if he would grant him a few minutes of his time.

"Young man, I usually have a big Texas steak with all the trimming," barked Sam.

"That will be fine, order whatever you want," replied Gray.

The real truth was his dinner was often a bowl of soup, a slice of bread and a cup of coffee. He couldn't remember the last time he had a good steak. But he was not about to tell the young man that.

Entering the dining room, Robert starts to sit down at the first empty table.

Sam walked past him to a table in the back, where he could see everyone entering the room.

Robert joined him at the table.

Sam said, "let's order before we talk. Tell you the truth. I'm so hungry I could eat the whole damn cow."

A waiter came to take their order.

Sam told him, "I want the biggest steak you got and all the trimmings. And plenty of black coffee. Okay young feller, what did you want to talk about?" asked Sam.

"Well, I would like to write a book about your experience as a gunfighter. I'm prepared to pay five hundred dollars in advance and five hundred dollars when the book is completed," stated Robert.

"Gosh, I don't know, I guess we can discuss it more after dinner. But to tell you the truth, I think you are wasting your money," remarked Sam.

At that moment, two men caught Sam's attention as they entered the hotel dining room. They didn't come to eat. Slowly, they start working their way toward his table. Sam's instinct told him something wasn't right. He slid his hand down and pulled out his revolver, and stuck it under his large napkin on the table, without Robert or the two men noticing it.

Robert was talking, but Sam was more focused on two men. He acted like he wasn't paying any attention to them.

Finally, they were at the table. "Hey Bart, ain't that the old washed-up gunfighter, everyone's talking about?"

Well dammit, sure 'nuff is, Dan. He don't look so tough to me. I heard he got his reputation by back-shooting 'em."

"Okay boys, you had your fun. Now go play somewhere else. Let us enjoy our meal," demanded Sam.

"Why don't you make us Old Man!" yelled Dan.

"I was wondering when you boys would get up enough courage for that. You sure I can't talk y'all boys out of this?" asked Sam.

"I'm gonna kill you, old man and everybody will know my name!" screamed Dan.

"You boys don't mind if I finish my apple pie and cup of coffee, do you?" asked Sam

"Just hurry up old man."

"Boy I'm full as a tick. You bovs couldn't ask for a better crowd to watch you get killed. Where the hell is my manners, boys, this is Robert, a reporter for the New York Sun. Now Boys, can't we just forget all this before someone gets hurt?" asked Sam.

"We're gonna kill you and that is a fact old man," stated Bart.

"You're just ate up with stupid ain't chya? Guess you know this ain't my first rodeo and I'm not planning it to be my last," explained Sam.

"Old Man, you better come out of that seat shooting or I will kill you where you set," brayed Dan.

"Tell you what sonny boy, a lot better men than you have tried it. Oh Robert, if I was you I would move."

Soon as Robert began moving, they drew their shootin' irons, expecting Sam to have stand to draw.

Sam fired his Colt from under the table, hitting both men in forehead. He placed the pistol on the table to wait for the sheriff who he knew was coming.

Robert was so shaken-up from experiencing the violence, he started vomiting his guts up seeing two men killed in front of him.

The sheriff walked in with his two deputies.

Sam raised his hands in the air to show everyone he wasn't resisting arrest.

"Alright Turley, you're going to jail."

"Wait a minute Sheriff, he did everything he could do to keep from killing them. They were going to kill him no matter what he did," explained Robert.

"And who are you. Trying to tell me my business."

"Sheriff. I'm just telling you, I witnessed the whole thing. Just like everyone else in this room. My name is Robert Gray with the New York Sun. I'm sending this story back to main office for print. I would like to write a favorable story about how you handled the situation," responded Robert.

"Well if you and everyone say it was self-defense. I have no choice, but to release Mr. Turley."

"Thank you Sheriff, I would like to stop by your office later to get an official statement for the paper if you don't mind?"

"No that be fine," answered the sheriff.

After the sheriff and his two deputies had some men remove the bodies and left, the crowd died down.

Sam thanked Robert for stepping in. "Matter of fact Robert, you really surprised me. That took some guts. If that sheriff had got me in one of his cells. Him and his two deputies would have made sure I didn't come out alive. He probably set-up those clowns, telling them if they killed me, they would be someone. If they had succeeded in killing me, him and his two deputies would have blown them apart with shotguns on their way to jail. Claiming they had tried to escape. I've seen that sheriff type before, it's control everybody or else. Those poor two jerks were dead when they walked in the cafe. They just weren't smart enough to know it. Where do you propose to do this interview, if I agree," asked Sam.

"What's wrong with right here, I'll get you a better room, next to mine. When you get tired, we will rest. But there is one thing, we need to get straight. Some of the words will need to be changed so the readers back east will understand the meaning. Well Robert, I guess you've been honest with me. Only fair I'm honest with you. I'm leaving right after my business with my lawyer is complete. The sheriff has ordered me out of town. Besides, I don't cotton to braying about one's own life so I guess I'll make tracks west. Thanks for dinner, So long Amigo."

Next morning Robert sat in his room feeling disappointed. Sam didn't take him up on his offer. When someone knocked on Robert's door.

Standing in the doorway was Sam. "Can I talk to you about your offer?" asked Sam.

"Sure, come in, sit down."

"Well Robert, I'm between a rock and hard spot. I will be up front with you. Things have changed since last night, to make it work for me, I would need the five hundred now, plus you would have to pay for my room and meals. But I will reimburse you for the room and meals off the balance of what's left of the five hundred."

Robert agreed, but was puzzled about what made Sam change his mind 'cause he wasn't interested a bit last night. But he knew better than to ask any questions. All Sam would say was a personal matter came up that needed his attention.

The truth was after dinner, Sam ran into an old friend's, grand-son who needed an operation on his eyes to keep him from going blind. The friend's grandson was checking out to go back home 'cause he didn't have the money for the operation. Sam agreed to tell his story to help pay for his friend's grandson's surgery. That was the least he could do for his friend, who took a bullet meant for him.

Here is Sam's story.

Leaving Texas, the two men crossed at the fork of the Red River where the water was shallow into Indian Territory. Not even noon yet, their bodies drenched from the sweat of the hot humid July day. One rode a big magnificent black stallion named Midnight standing close to sixteen hands, with a thick neck, brawn body and having an amazing mind for a horse. The rider rode tall in the saddle. Handsome in a rugged sort of way with high cheek-bones, olive skin, dark black hair with grit for his twenty plus years. His name was Sam Turley, son of Cole Turley, the gunfighter. Sam's father was a mixture of race, being, Irish, Black and Ute Indian. Sam's mother was a beautiful Cherokee woman who was murdered and raped when Sam was a young boy. Sam began breaking horses on his father's and uncle Luke's ranch in Texas.

Deciding to take some time off, he was heading to his father's sister's ranch outside of Tahlequah. She had raised him after his mother's death. Then, he figured on heading to Colorado, to visit his father, Cole and his wife, also, his half brothers and sisters. Sam was turning out to look a lot like his father, Cole, in a lot of ways. Fast with a gun, with either hand and he enjoyed horses. His father, Cole, had given him Midnight, who was the grandson out of the famous black stallion Blackjack.

The other man was Butch Lee in his forties, short, big pot-belly with gray hair, what hair he had.

They were two strange looking hombres traveling together, but with times like they were, it was better to have a companion along. Both had worked on Sam's uncle's ranch. When Butch learned Sam was heading north, he decided to go with him to his home in Kansas.

Sam being good with a gun, knowing the land, besides he liked and trusted Sam.

On the third day out, they came upon a large herd of longhorn cattle heading up the Shawnee Trail, on their way to Kansas or Missouri market they figured.

After getting past all the dust and smell of the herd, they met up with the trail boss. A slender built man, brown hair, around thirty years, with a mustache, face, weather-worn, with a pale blue bandana around his neck. His name was Bob Woods from Abilene, with a crew of fifteen men.

Butch remarked he was surprised to see a herd of longhorns on the Shawnee Trail anymore. Cattle drives usually took the Christum Trail.

Grinnin', the trail boss said, "Is that a fact. Rumor is, the stock-pens are over-filled in Kansas. Some cattlemen made a deal with the government to deliver beef to Fort Gibson and the Cherokee Nation. He apologized for not offering them a hot meal, but their cook drowned crossing the Red River. The river got its name from the red soil it carried downstream and was notorious for the quicksand it held. Many people had drowned across it.

Butch, sensing he might have offended the trail boss, offered to fix a hot evening meal for the crew. Him being a ranch cook. If Sam didn't mind, they'd stay the night.

When some of cowboys came in for their evening meal, one cowhand upon hearing Sam's father was Cole Turley tried to pick a gunfight with him.

Giving the cowboy, a chilling stare, Sam told him to leave him along, unless he wanted to see what hell looked like.

The young cowboy laughed nervously, backing off while Sam went back to brush his big stallion. After everyone had eaten their evening meal and the camp fire died down. Butch walked over where Sam was laying, staring up at all the shiny bright stars.

"Hey Sam, the trail boss offered me a job as their cook. I was thinking about taking it, if you don't mind."

"Hell Butch, it sounds like a pretty good ideal to me. Good Luck to you."

Butch started to leave, but suddenly turned around telling Sam, "watch out for that one cowboy, he's out to get you."

Morning came early, Sam washed the sleep from his eyes. Smelling hot coffee brewing, biscuits cooking.

Watching Butch stirring a big pot of Texas butter gravy made with flour, hot water and fried steak grease. Nothing like a hot breakfast before the start of the day.

Sipping on his second cup of hot coffee, he saddled his big black stallion. A voice yelled for him to turn around, Sam knew right away it was, the young cowboy.

Sneering with a grin, the young cowboy said, "I heard you're Cole Turley's bastard son."

Sam studied the young cowboy's face, about his age, blond hair, blue-grayish eyes, slender built, wearing chaps with a gun strapped down like he knew how to use it. Amused Sam said, "that what they say? Why don't you tell me something I don't know? Ain't got time for this."

Sam turned back around to leave, trying everything possible from killing the young cowboy. But the cowboy yelled, "your mother's a whore.

Sam could not walk away from that. Turning back around, Sam noticed the rest of the crew quietly watching. Sam announced, "I have never in my life seen anyone in such a hurry to die. You can either apologize or draw your gun anytime."

The cowboy's gun had not cleared his holster before a bullet struck him in the shoulder. Sam strolled over, where the cowboy lay bleeding, in a lot of pain. Sam informed him to learn something from this experience, because he was slower than molasses in January. "I could have easily killed you."

Sam mounted his stallion heading north toward Tahlequah. Weather conditions began to change fast, Big dark clouds hung low rolling in the sky, visible lighting, whirling wind blowing hard against the big stallion. Sam needed to seek shelter from the storm and possibly of a tornado coming. He had witnessed the damage a tornado could cause.

The Ouachita Mountains lay ahead lined with hidden caverns and ravines. If Sam could make it there, he could hold up until the storm blew over. He hunted the area as a young boy. One such place was Robbers Cave running back into the mountain some forty feet. Scenic hilly woodland in the San Bois Mountains, it was a haven for outlaws. With its massive boulders and clear spring water. Since there was no local or state law existing in the territory. Outlaws were reported hiding out there.

The James gang, the Youngers, Daltons and Belle Starr gangs. It definitely was no place for strangers, but Sam didn't have a choice. He needed to find a place quick, until the storm blew over. Besides, his big black stallion needed to rest. Coming up around the bend of trail near a stream of water, stood a log cabin, near-by was a barn.

Sam rode up to the cabin, but before he could dismount, someone demanded to know what his intentions were. Sam stated he was looking for shelter from the storm and willing to pay.

Slowly, the door opened, and a rifle stuck out. A man's voice yelled he could sleep in the barn for a dollar. "That would be in advance and you better be gone by morning."

Sam held out a dollar while a young Indian girl ran out to get it. Turning Midnight toward the barn just as the rain begin coming down. The barn smelled of musty, damp odors of mildew where previous rain had leaked on some hay. Different objects lay about on the dirt floor of the barn. Signs of neglect shown throughout the rusty-looking old barn.

Unsaddling his stallion, Sam placed his gear upon some hay. Making himself a place to sleep, then brushing his horse down and giving the stallion some oats to eat. He found an old wooden bucket to sit on while he cleaned his guns. Sam had brought himself two pearl-handled 1873 Colt Peacemaker 45 pistols before he left Texas. Before day-break, the rain was still coming down hard, but the wind had quit blowing. Suddenly, Midnight began nickering and kicking his hoofs into the barn wall. Sam whispered to calm Midnight down. He heard the barn door squeaking open. He rolled in the hay with his pistols drawn. Gun-shots rang out hitting his bed-roll. He fired twice hitting the gun-man standing in the barn door. Sam reached for a lantern nearby, lit it checking the body. A whopping tallow of man with a full-grown beard lay there dead. Praising and patting Midnight for warning him of the danger. Seeing a light in the cabin, he headed toward it.

With pistols drawn, Sam kicked in the cabin door. The cabin was one huge room with a large rock fireplace in the corner. Two young, frightened Indian women stood by the rock fireplace. One, a gorgeous, well-built woman with a chesty breast, long firm legs, coal black hair down her back.

He asked her who was the man he'd just killed and why did he try to kill him.

"He murdered our folks and was planning on selling us to some outlaws. He figured on killing you for your horse and guns. Glad the bastard is dead. He's a son of Walt Reed, a vicious, blood-thirsty old Irish-man. He has seven sons with thirty to forty men riding under him. Old man Reed, a greed, cold hearted killer. Raised his boys to be just like him. They say he killed his own wife 'cause he got tired of looking at her. Things got pretty hot in Missouri for them with the blue-bellys, always chasing them. So he moved his operation to Indian Territory, where there's no white man law. I was forced to listen to all the bragging about his stupid family. I know one thing for sure, them boys are plum scared of that crazy old man." She asked Sam if they could travel with him to Tahlequal where they had kin.

Sam learned her name was Grace and her sister' name was Sue Ellen, the girl who came out to take his dollar.

Crack of dawn, they were on the trail head north.

In a clearing on the side of the mountain Sam halted Midnight to watch over fifty wild mustangs running wild and free. To Sam, it was a marvelous sight to witness. Sam had trained Midnight to perform properly as his horse. But when he was breaking horses at the ranch, he let Midnight run free to breed the mares.

Pushing onward across a rocky trail, finally stopping around noon to eat some beef jerky and rest beside a spring of cool water.

Sam noticed three riders galloping toward them at a fast pace from the south. Too hot of a day to be pushing horses that hard. Sam told the two girls to ride on while he stayed behind. Grace told him maybe he should ride on. If they got them back, maybe it would be enough. Sam tied his stallion to a clump of trees. She pleaded with Sam to ride on. But by that time, it was too late. Sam faced the three outlaws with a determined look on his face. One rider with long brownish hair, light blue eyes, a scar above his left eye stepped down from his pale brown horse.

He was wearing a Stetson hat, with a woman's garter around the band of hat. Looking taller than his medium build. He wore his gun like a person highly skilled in use of a gun. He said, "you got balls with back-bone boy, going up against three desperadoes. Either that or you are dumb as a box of rocks. Last chance to ride away. You two butt-heads stay out of this. This boy's got sand, something you two will never have. I'm counting to three, you better be ready."

Sam was aware he probably was facing the fastest gun, he ever had. The two butt-head men stepped off their horses. The two looked grimy in appearance compared to the long haired stranger. Dead silence was in the air, then 123 sound of leather being slapped, guns blazing, then the sound of bullet tearing into his flesh, staggering to stay-up, watching the gunman fall to the ground. Blood ran down Sam's left arm soaking his shirt. Catching a glimpse of the two outlaws drawing their guns. Sam sprung around, shooting the back-slouch yellow-bellys. Watching them hit the ground. Time only to shoot to kill before they kill him.

Gunsmoke cleared with only gun-power smell left in the air.

The women looked astonished to see the outlaws' bodies laying on the ground. Breaking the silence, Grace commented, "oh my God. You're bleeding. Luckly, it did not hit a bone." Grace stopped the bleeding and started wrapping up his arm.

Sue Ellen began checking the bodies for valuables. She howled, "hey, this one got a five-hunderd dollar reward on him. This is Bill Duck who rode with the James gang. They raided a Mexican caravan of gold bullion belonging to Mexican general. A posse was hot on their tail, so rumor has it, so Jesse buried the gold somewhere on Cache River in the Wichita mountains. Wait until people hear about this?"

Curious, Sam eyed her saying he did not need a reputation like that. If the sisters want to claim the reward fine, but leave his name out of it. His last name gave him enough problems.

"Besides, you probably could use the money to get a fresh start."

Grace was starting to feel a strong affection toward this tall, handsome man named Sam Turley. Oh, she knew he was wild as a big Texas twister, but she could not help herself. To complicate matters worse, her sister Sue Ellen was eyeing him also. Staying until Sam was fit to travel.

They tied down the bodies on their horses and continued north. Next morning, Sam mentioned he needed to stop at Fort Gibson Fort before he went to Tahlequal. He promised his dad and uncle, he would check on a cousin stationed there in the 10th Cavalry.

"Oh you have a cousin who's an officer in the 10th Cavalry?" asked Grace.

"No he's a private who I have never met," answered Sam.

"But all the troops are negroes in the 10th Cavalry," Grace explained.

Sam grinned saying, "they are call'em Buffalo Soldiers. I am of Cherokee, Ute, Irish and Negro blood. "Sam watched for a reaction from Grace's face before he spoke again. "Maybe someone can verity the bodies of the outlaws, so we will not have to take them to Tahelequal."

Next day around noon, they arrived at the stockade. The fort was full of soldiers constantly on patrol engaging in keeping the peace among the hostiles Indians. The fort was built on a gently sloping hill over-looking the Grand River. Within sight of the point where the Grand, Verdigris and Arkansas Rivers unite to form the greater Arkansas River. Besides a barracks for the men, there was a guard house, an officer's quarters and a small building to cook in, next to the mess hall was a hospital. The stockade where the horses and mules were kept was down the hill close to the river dock. Twenty-five thousand tons of freight would be transferred annually between the fort and New Orleans on steamboats.

Most of the time, duty at the fort was dull being out in the middle of nowhere.

Two lovely-looking women showing up made the fort come alive. Sam left the women with a handful of soldiers while he went to visit his cousin who was unfortunately in the guard house for fighting. His cousin, a black man in his twentys, muscular built, a witty grin, an attitude that attracted people. His problems all began when he joined the Army.

A night of heavy drinking and encouragement from a 10th Cavalry sergeant to enlist in the army. Something he truly regretted doing because he was not used to men he didn't like ordering him around. Next morning, after chow, Sam took the women to meet the company commander.

Maybe with a little persuading, the girl could get rid of the outlaws' bodies and receive the reward and be on their way.

Colonel Bell, a heavy-set man, thinning white hair, blood-shot eyes sat behind his desk, going over a dispatch he had just received. Disappointed that his orders for a transfer back east had not come in.

Afterwards, the sergeant took Sam and the girls to see him. The room was small in size, no windows, an office desk cluttered with several objects. The colonel's uniform looked wrinkled like he had slept in it. His pistols and sword hung on the wall beside his hat. A faint smell of alcohol mixed with body odor was in the air. Sam explained the situation about the outlaws. The colonel could authorize payment if he received their three horses and saddles. The reward money would be delayed a week or two until the bodies were positively identified.

Sam said that would be fine as long his cousin, Clay Miller got out the guard house with a three day pass. Sam was letting the colonel know he was not going to be bullied. He was getting something out of deal or taking the bodies on to Tahequal.

The colonel talked over the situation with the sergeant. Since Private Miller's time in the stockade was almost up, the colonel agreed. Next day, the weather was perfect for a picnic. The wind was gently blowing a cool breeze. White fluffy clouds drifting high in the light blue sky.

Sam, Clay, and the girls decided to look for a secluded area down close to river for a picnic. Sam spread out a blanket, watching the magnificent butterflys, floating among the giant sunflowers. Clay and Sue Ellen immediately lost interest in the picnic. Their bodies entwined together began strolling to the river edge. Once there, they shucked off their clothes to swim in the cool water. Kissing and grabbing each other bodies. Clay pulled Sue Ellen onto the grass riverbank where they soon disappeared. Sam glanced over toward Grace's luscious lovely body. She was watching her baby sister and Clay. Furious, she looked over at Sam implying she was not that easy, besides she couldn't swim.

Sam lay back on the army blanket, closed his eyes imagining her with those big firm breasts, long black hair running against the wind. The only thing Sam was getting today was maybe some fried chicken. In Clay's three day pass, Clay and Sue Ellen became inseparable. Grace asked Sam to accompany her to the trading post a few miles outside the fort. Entering the spacious log building they encountered a foul horrible smell. Discovering the smell came from a giant buffalo hunter. Having a full long black beard, matte hair, devastating cold reddish dark eyes, fists bigger than cantaloupes, body solid as a rock. Used to taking what he wanted and his eyes were on Grace.

He started to force his intentions on Grace, not caring Sam was standing beside her. When she complained, he laughed at her. Sam clenched his fists hitting him hard across the jaw-bone of his face. Turning his attention toward Sam, his left fist caught Sam on the chin, leaving his whole head ringing with pain. Leaving the taste of blood in his mouth, Sam absorbed the pain and swung back.

The Buffalo hunter's fists keep pounding Sam's body until a big roundhouse blow send Sam to the floor.

Laughing, bending over, grabbing Sam's body, braying, "when I'm done with you, there won't be enough left of you to snore."

Grace grabbed a big black iron skillet off the shelf, striking the Buffalo hunter repeatedly across the back of his head. The big savage Buffalo hunter fell like a giant oak across Sam's body. Blood covered the big iron skillet. Grace tossed it aside, and helped Sam to his feet.

Sam still wobbling asked, am I dead?"

Panicky Grace said, "I don't know, but please, let us get out of here fast."

A few days later, Sam was ready to continue on to Tahlequal. He figured Grace wasn't going on since the reward money had not arrived yet and her sister was staying with Clay at the fort. He had his big black stallion saddled, telling Clay good-bye. When Grace asked, "are we finally leaving?"

Puzzled Sam explained it was a long hard two days. Riding over narrow trail with steep hills and some deep ruts. If she was planning on going with him, she better quit pussy-footing around. Zestful she replied, "I been waiting on you since day-break." She returned with her horse, plus a mule pack ready to go. The road to Tahlequal was rocky and slow going with the sun in their eyes.

They stopped on Fourteen Mile Creek to rest from the boiling heat. Sam observed Grace, washing her lovely face. Usually, he never had a problem with women until Grace happened along. Sam remarked if they headed due east from Fourteen Creek, there was a cabin where an old man lives. Sam knew him since he was a boy. He would let them stay the night.

Brilliant red-orange sun was beaming fiery heat waves against the western blue sky. Burning into their back as they continued their journey east.

Reaching the cabin built of native rock and an awesome fireplace. It rested among two large cottonwood trees. Two horses were tied-up out in front, one a splendid Appaloosa the other a bay. Two men exited the cabin, one holding a bottle of whiskey. One man was medium built, but he looked wild and woolly, had fair skin, his hat pulled down over his ears to protect his light skin and red hair, few freckles from the sun. He wore a black leather vest, his pant's legs tucked inside his fancy boots with silver spurs, he was built like cocky snake on stilts with his gun dangling out.

The other man, short with long greasy brown hair, a whopping belly, ugly as a mud-fence, a foul smell to him, a boot-licker for sure.

Sam dismounted his stallion, "howdy, is the old man around?"

"He's dead just like you're fixing to be. Unless you leave those fancy guns, black stallion and that good-looking gal here for me to play with," claimed the arrogant, bloodthirsty red-headed stranger.

"Damn Mister, you sure don't leave a person with much," Sam stated.

The short man spouted off, "if I was you Mister, I would get to walking, that's Red Reed, the gunfighter."

Sam asked, "just which one of you blowhard bastards killed the old man or did it take both of yellow-belly cowards?"

Red yelled, "Hoss, get ready to meet your maker."

The fat weasel man drew his pistol, also, to fire.

In a flash, Sam shot both men in the gut, a slow painful death. He put both his guns back in his holster, taunt the conceited fools, before they could hit the ground to die. Sam stripped both men of their clothes. Dragging their worthless naked bodies to a deep dark ravine, throwing their bodies into it.

Grace had never seen Sam act in this weird manner and it kind of scared her.

Sam buried the old man out back under some pine trees. He started drinking the old man's whiskey at the kitchen table.

Grace sat quietly at the table listening to tales of the Old Man.

Sam never knew the old man's real name. Some say he had been a outlaw with a reward on his head. He asked Sam to just call him Old Man. It was an Irish custom to have a wake to honor one's life. Sam was honoring the Old Man. Just like it was Indian's custom to show disrespect to ones who were untrustworthy like he had the two bodies. Sam asked Grace to join him in a toast to the old man's life. Either one hadn't had much to eat that day, so the whiskey burned going down. Sam could not remember how much he drank, just that Grace kept up with him. He woke-up naked in bed with one hell of a hangover, curious how he got there. Laying beside him was Grace, butt naked. He wondered just what he had missed. He snatched her glorious body, waking her. Their hot wet lips locked together producing steamy passionate kisses, hands rubbing each other bodies in forbidden places. Their hot sweating bodies came together. Trembling, gasping for air, she moaned with pleasure, desiring more. They spent most of the day in bed, pleasing each other. Only getting up to eat some food. Crawling back in bed to begin. When they finally crawled out of bed, both were definitely in love. Finally, making their way toward town

Sam not wanting Grace to leave asked if she would like to meet his aunt Sarah and see where he grew up at. Sam never took any girls around his family. He had been with a lot of women, but this one was special. She wasn't conceited about her beautiful looks. She, also, had an inner beauty about her. She was trustworthy, adventurous, and had caring ways. Sure, her outer-body looks was what Sam noticed first. But he wouldn't have brought her home unless he had not fallen in love with all of Grace.

Reaching the ranch, Aunt Sarah welcomed Sam home. Her and Grace seemed to enjoy each other's company.

Telling Sam his mother's place was in good condition if she ever wanted to see it sometime, but she would understand if she did not. Thinking they might need some private time together. Sarah and Sam's mother, Ruth, were best friends. Ruth had loved her home so much and Sarah really want Sam to see how she kept Ruth's memory alive. Grace helped Aunt Sarah cook the evening meal while Sam tended to the horses. Exhausted from the hot summer heat

Uncle Lee rode up on a sorrel horse. He'd been working up on the north range fixing fence. Still tall and slim, but his hair was gray. Lee always treated Sam like a son he never had. After the evening meal, the women did the dishes. While Sam and Lee sat outside on the porch listening to a lone wolf howling in the distance. Gazing upon a million bright stars hanging low in the evening night. Something Sam never got tired of admiring.

Breaking the silence, he asked Lee if he heard about the Indian war around Palo Duro on the Red River.

Lee shook his head, saying, "we don't get any news unless we get to town. But back April 15 what they called the Going Snake Massacre happened. A part Cherokee name of Proctor shot a white man name of Kecterson in the head, seriously wounding him. Then he shot Polly Beck, a beautiful Cherokee woman killing her. Some say the victim, Polly Beck, was a love interest to Proctor. It seems Kesterson had been married to Proctor's sister and abandoned her for Polly Beck. Kecterson got the local U.S. Commissioner to issue a warrant for Proctor, if the Cherokee court failed to convict him. At a school house outside of Tahlequah where they were having the trial, eight lawmen approached the building. Several Cherokee exited the building and began firing at the Deputy Marshals. When it was over, eight lawmen were dead, three Cherokee dead and six wounded. The next day, the Cherokee jury acquitted Proctor. Why they didn't just let the Cherokee handle their own affairs beat me. Eleven men killed.

Sam stood up, stretched his body remarking, "it's not good news for the Indians. They been crowded out by the killing of the buffalo and progress. Buffalo Hunters moved in with the expanding of railroad and the market for hides and meat back east. They are killing all the buffalo. The Indian's way of life is gone and it's sad. I will be heading to Colorado to see Dad, but before I leave, I will help you around here. I got to take Grace to her kin-folks also."

Chuckling Lee rose to his feet, took out his pipe, lit it, took a puff, enjoying the smell of pipe before he answered. "Sam, you might know horses, but vou sure don't know women. That girl's got her eyes set on you to marry her. Oh don't worry, it happens to the best of us. One day you will wake-up and wonder just how in the hell did you make it without her."

Next morning everyone was setting around the kitchen table drinking coffee and enjoying each other's company.

While a thunderstorm was blowing in outside, the clouds begin rolling across the gloomy sky. Grace hinted it might be good day to visit Sam's mom's home. Her big beautiful brown eyes danced with excitement. Aunt Sarah agreed. Sam quivered with the ideal of returning where his mother was murdered. His condemn for his grandfather only grew more sour with time. Ruth's father's a loathsome person that took advantage of her depression. Her spirt broken and her heart crushed when it was reported Cole was killed at Gettysburg.

He controlled her by threating to sell her son Sam to work the silver mines in Mexico. Blaming her for dis-honoring his blood line with what he called an Irish-nigger child. He had secretly sent Ruth away upon learning of her pregnancy almost seventeen years ago to live with distant relatives.

No one knew about Sam until Ruth's father let her return home thinking Cole was dead. And Ruth was inheriting a ranch from Cole's step grandmother. Under the condition of the will, she could only sell the property to Cole's family. Cole's grandmother knew Ruth's father wanted to get his greedy hands on the ranch. So she put certain clauses in her will to protect Ruth. Hearing of Cole's death, her father forced her into a marriage with a drunkard wife-beater. Ruth was raped and murdered by three men. Her so call husband was in town getting drunk. She lived long enough to give important information about her killers. Cole returned home to discover, he had a sixteen year old son named Sam and Ruth was murdered.

Cole revenged her death killing her so called husband, plus two of his paid friends. Tracking down her killers and by accident finding a fortune in gold. He shared the fortune with his family. Buying ranches in Texas, Colorado and more land in Oklahoma. His reputation as a gunfighter was well known, something he could not live down, much as he tried. Cole knew he had to teach Sam how to handle a gun, if not, someone would kill him, just because he was Cole's son. Cole wasn't a vindictive person only when someone harmed a person he loved.

Sam decided he needed to face the past and move on.

Going to his mother's home was in the right direction. Arriving at the gate, he halted Midnight to gaze upon the place. The ranch house was a large white two-story home over-looking the valley below. A spacious barn and corrals some five hundred feet from the house. A water-well stood to the left of house so not to spoil the view from the huge front porch. Out-house was in back some two hundred feet.

Sam took a deep breath, walked in side. He noticed the house was full of furniture with some of his mother's personal things lying around. In the living room, stood a enormous sand-stone fire-place with impressive decorations on the wall. Oil lamps set on two tables. His Aunt Sarah had built a shine to honor her friend.

Outside the rain slowly begin to come down. Sam's mind was being flooded with fond memories of his mother. He had totally neglected the horses. Grabbing the reins, he led them to the barn with Grace beside him. He noticed Grace shivering from the cold rain when he unsaddled Midnight. He retrieved a blanket from his gear. Handing her the blanket, he continued to unsaddle her horse. She removed her wet clothes, wrapping herself up in the blanket. Smelling the sweet fresh cut hay, stored there by Lee, hearing the horses snorting. birds chirping in the hay loft, the rain hitting tin roof.

Sam finished caring for the horses. Spreading out another blanket, he lay down on the fresh hay. His mind wandered fondly remembering his mother. Rain beat harder against the tin roof. Grace lay down beside him sharing her blanket.

She removed his wet clothes.

Huddling to stay warm. Pounding of their hearts beat exciting like the cold rain outside. Their bodies became aroused to feel and smell of each other body. Their trembling bodies thrust together making hard fantastic love again and again.

Bodies became wedged together until their bodies became complete exhausted. If this kept up, "we will never get you to your kin-folks."

Suspicious, Grace eyed him, "if you are try to tell me to go I will."

Fondly looking her ravishing body over, Sam chuckled, "just the oppose, I was trying figure a way for you to stay."

The days became weeks, the weeks into months. Their love continued to grow. Sam was not ready for that final commitment of marriage. But he didn't want to lose her either. He started noticing Grace gaining weight, have morning sickness. He wondered if she was pregnant, so he asked her. Grace a proud woman not want to tie Sam down. Answered, "no, I must have swallowed a watermelon seed."

It was about time she left for her kin-folks. Affectionately, Sam whispered in Grace's ear, "You are someone to ride the river with, I would be honored to have you for my wife, if you would have me. A week later they were married, living at his mom's place. Sam was working with Lee on the ranch. It was the happiest time Sam ever knew.

About a month later, around sunset they were just sitting down for their evening meal, when ten heavily armed men rode up to the house. They formed a half circle around the front porch. Sam strapped on his guns, stepped out on the porch. An older man in his late fortys, with grayish-red hair, a little on the heavy side. He looked like he had done more drinking than work. He was setting on a large strawberry roan horse. He asked if he was Sam Turley.

Standing firm against the cabin wall, Sam nodded his head that he was, not liking his odds.

"I'm Jake Reed, came with my brother and some kin-folks to revenge my two brother's deaths."

Sam explained how it happened. "One of your brothers killed an old man and tried me in a fair fight. Other one tried to bush-whack me and killed an old Indian couple."

Amused, Jake stepped off the roan, jawing, "that sounds just like them."

The rest of the men stepped off their horses.

Fearlessly Sam assured Jake, he would be the first one killed.

Jake in an attempt to shake-up Sam and catch him off guard. He boasted about killing his cousin and torturing his wife's sister to death. I must admit it took us three whole days before she broke down to tell us."

Suddenly without any warning, Grace rushed on to the porch with a double-barrel shot-gun. Taking aim, she saw the grin turn to panic in Jake's eyes. She pulled both triggers. The blast knock Jake's body back a good ten feet almost removing his head. In an instant, Sam drew both guns, blazing away with bodies falling. Seconds later, Grace took a bullet and another one in the chest. Sam rushed to her side, reaching her only to be hit by a hail of bullets.

One bullet grazed his head, knocking him unconscious. Their bodies soaked in blood started running across the porch.

The one's who survived the gun battle torched the house and barn. They loaded up their wounded and dead and headed out. Lee was sitting out on porch smoking his pipe when he noticed the fire in the distance. He swiftly rushed to the scene in time to pull their bodies from the fire. Only to find Grace dead and Sam in a bad way. The hope of Sam surviving was very slim since he had lost so much blood. He'd be lucky if he made it through the night.

Against all odds, Sam slowly started to improve. Over a week later, he gained conscious only to ask about Grace. Sadly, upon learning of Grace's fate, teardrops slowly ran down Sam's face. He promised to revenge her death and his unborn child. It would be two months before Sam started recovering from the wounds to his body. The bullet that grazed his forehead was a different matter causing severe headaches. Sometimes followed by black-out spells and seizures. Sam's family started rumors he had died. Keeping the Reed family from coming back to finish the job of killing him. They even put up a tombstone next to Grace's grave. When news reached Cole, he came to Sam's aid. Sam told his father he appreciated his help, but this was something he needed to take care of himself.

Cole completely understood, but his son was not physically or mentally ready for the task yet. He needed his mind focused and his body to heal. He had a long way to go before he fully recovered from his injuries. Eventually, Sam persuaded his father to return home to oversee a cattle drive going to Montana. He had a lot folks counting on him to deliver the cattle. But Cole still would not leave until Sam promised at Grace's grave to stay at the ranch until he returned. Cole's friend, Ike Johnston who came with him from Colorado agreed to stay and help out. Sam had never met anyone quite like Ike. A tall and lean black man, who had the saddest brown eyes, with a steel look of authority. He hardly spoke a word, his reflexes were quick and accurate.

Sam told his father he didn't need a babysitter to watch over him.

Cole stared hard, his face turning red with rage telling his son. "That is my friend, you will treat him with the respect he deserves and appreciate the help he is offering you. You can learn a lot about life from him. There is no one faster with a gun than him."

Cole left for Colorado the next morning. Sam spent the day by Grace's grave grieving. He felt like someone ripped out his heart, roots and all. He had nothing left, but hatred and revenge. Sam stood beside Grace's grave weeping when someone said, "you can only grieve so much for someone. Life goes on, either you live for them or you die."

Slowly Sam turned to face Ike with hatred in his eyes. "What the hell would you know about it."

Ike stared with them big sad brown eyes, "You think Boy, you're the only one who ever lost someone? If you want to get revenge for her killing. I'm here to teach you, but don't waste my time."

Sam stayed behind observing the magnificent sunset resting between two small green mountains. Gigantic fire-ball of stunning colors of orange, yellow and ruby red against a lavender sky. The ground slowly gobbled-up the beautiful site until only darkness was present.

Sam spent the night tossing and turning in bed but was up at day-break.

Ike was sitting at the kitchen table staring at his coffee cup. Sam walked over and sat across the table from Ike.

"I need to apologize for the way I treated you. My father said I could learn a lot from you. I am ready to start whenever you are."

Ike worked with Sam building up his muscles, working on his gun skills, most important was mind control. Ike said he needed to function like a brilliant killing machine. Ike still remained a big mystery to everyone except Cole. However, once Sam did walk up on Ike while he was washing up. His back was a washboard of scars. Whoever was responsible for the beating. You can be assured they paid dearly for it. Ike didn't take anything from nobody. By the end of summer, Sam had developed a strong respect for the man. If Ike ever needed Sam, he would be there for him. Sam finally realized what his father meant calling Ike a trusty trojan.

The beginning of fall, the tree leaves started turning gorgeous colors.

Ike remarked he had taught Sam all he could. The rest was up to Sam to deal with revenge.

Ike took a short leisurely walk that day. Down by the big oak trees to enjoy the fall scenery view.

Leaning-up against a big oak tree Ike encountered a flashback of his past. Dredging up old memories of distress, sorrow and guilt. An emotional time, triggering the memory to the smell, taste and pain of that time. Reliving the experience of a nightmare. Traveling across Texas by wagon with his wife and two boys. Five shaggy men appeared. Ike tried to fight them off, but they strung him up to a big oak tree. One of men got out a bull whip and began whipping him across the back. They shot and killed his two boys. They took turns, raping his wife making him watch the ordeal, then killing her. They had beat and whip him so much, they left him for dead hanging by his arms. He would have if Cole had not ridden by the next morning to cut him down.

After Cole buried Ike's wife and two sons under a giant oak tree. He took Ike to a nearby cabin. Sending a farmer's son to fetch a doctor while him and his Indian friend Sky-Hawk tracked the five men. Learning the identity of the five men and knowing they were in a permanent location on their ranch. Cole started to leave. His Indian friend, Sky-Hawk didn't like the ideal of him leaving. Cole asked, "if this happened to your family, wouldn't you like to be the one to revenge their murders. If he dies, we will return to get justice for him the Indian way."

Sky-Hawk nodded in agreement.

The farmer was out plowing the field with a mule that wasn't cooperating when they reached the cabin. The doctor was loading his buggy to leave. Cole asked about Ike's condition, only to be told. He didn't treat the likes of him. Cole calmly pulled out his revolver. Stating; "You can either treat him or I will blow your damn head off. Now it don't make a damn to me, either way, you call it."

Laughing, Sky-Hawk dismounted his horse patting the doctor on the back. "Go on Doc, call Cole's bluff."

Hastily the Doctor returned to the cabin. In a couple days, Cole and Sky-Hawk moved Ike to a different location to keep him safe. Ike slowly began to recover from the beating with only one thing on his mind. First thing Ike needed to learn was patience, if Ike was to have any chance at all with five men who murdered his family.

Cole felt an obligation to teach him the art of being a gunfighter and how to control his emotions. "Because your opponent will use every trick to slow down your draw."

In time, Ike was ready for the showdown. Round-up time would be a good time to catch all five men together before driving their cattle to market, probably Dodge City.

Cole, Sky-Hawk and Ike rode into the camp. They stood by Ike's side to keep everyone out except the five men who inflicted Ike's pain. Fifteen ranch hands stood between them and the five men.

Disgust and anger showed in Ike's eyes. He was finally facing the five men who had dealt him so much pain. One of five men was Lee Bannett. He owned the largest ranch around. A real pompous-ass person. A medium size man with curly brown hair, side-burns and a mustache. He fancied himself a bit of gunfighter and a lady's man in his fancy sliver spurs. Everyone called him

Little-Big Man behind his back, but to his face he was known as Mr. B. He was the one who beat Ike with the bull-whip and was the leader of pack. With fifteen men backing him up, he became cocky. He started laughing and boasting about his deed. Taunting Ike with how much he enjoyed his wife and killing his two boys.

Ike just stared at him showing no emotions.

He took that as sign of weakness and fear. Bragging to Cole, "if you two men will stay out of this, I will take care of this nigger myself."

Cole smiled, saying, "he is all yours. But frankly, I don't think you're man enough for the job. But we will stand down, just as long your men do the same.

Little-Big Man ordered the fifteen men to stay out. Thinking to himself, this is going to be a walk in the park. Grinning he faced Ike, saying, "anytime you're man enough."

"No," Ike said, "cowards always go first."

He began to draw his gun when a bullet tore off his left ear. Looking down the barrel of Ike's gun. "Why don't you try again, but this time, try be a little faster," stated Ike.

Fear began to show in the man's eyes for he knew Ike was toying with him., but he had no choice. This time the bullet tore off Bannett's right ear. His proud face began swelling up the size of a watermelon. He looked a pitiful sight. Blood spattered across his face running down his body onto the ground. Begging for mercy, seeing the swiftness of Ike guns. Ike had deliberately shot off his ears. He wanted the self-centered bastard to knows day of reckoning was here. Cole advised the fifteen men, "unless you want to die for these five men, you better walk away. We came here to die if necessary to see this man get justice."

One brave cowboy gripped his gun handle saying, "you can't get us all."

"That is true, but I will take some with me starting with you," stated Cole. "And I will, also, take some with me," Sky-Hawk spoke up. "It will be a great honor to die with the famous gunfighter, Cole Turley. My people will talk about this for years to come," remarked Sky-Hawk.

"Alright, face the deadly consequences or walk away," barked Cole.

Upon learning the truth, hearing the name of Cole Turley, the cowboys began to leave the five men to face their own fate. Little-Big Man begged for them to stay. Offering large sums of money if they would help him.

A couple of rowdy young cowboys hearing the amount stopped in their tracks. Turning around to face Cole, one young lanky cowboy stated, "that's a lot of money."

Cole studied his face, before he spoke. "It is, only if you live to spend it. I sure hope you are not fixing to do something stupid. I sure would hate to kill you," explained Cole.

"Maybe so, but I don't like the ideal of backing down from no one. Even if you are the high and mighty Cole Turley."

"Who said you was backing down? We are only here to see our friend get justice and see that no one interferes with him. What happens today is between him and these five men. How would you feel, if it was your family?" asked Cole.

The young lean cowboy pondered a few seconds. Pushing back his hat, revealing his long red-blondish hair. Oh hell--couldn't enjoy the money knowing that. He motioned for his comrades to leave.

All this time, Ike never took his eyes off the five men.

Rattled the four men tried to put all the blame on Little-Big Man.

"No one forced you to be a party to it!" yelled Ike. "You are nothing but a bunch of ten-cent men with a tear squeezer tale."

Hastily, Little Big Man drew his iron to fire, but slick as grease, Ike shot the gun from his hand. Then placing a bullet in each leg causing him to fall to his knees. "Which of you cowards wants to be next?"

A lanky man in his fortys spoke. "Think I speak for all of us. A huge mistake was made. We are willing to sit you up in your own ranch and give you money to get you started. We know it will never take the place of your family."

"Damn, you would do that for me. I always wanted to have my own place, sounds great," Ike replied. "What's your name?"

"It's Harry Dill, I hope someday you will find in your heart to forgive us."

"Well Harry, what are we going to do about him?" pointing his peacemaker toward Little-Big Man?"

"Kill him, it was all his ideal anyway. He looks a little peaked anyway. Besides, he has been top hog at the trough too damn long. Time to get rid of the four-flusher." Harry grinned to himself thinking, "I sure slicker him and with Lee gone that would make him the biggest toad in the puddle."

"Dammit Harry, the only problem I got is. How do I know if I can trust you? Now if you was to kill Bannett yourself, maybe I could trust you."

Ike handed Harry a pistol. Glancing around, Harry asked, "where did your pardners go?"

"Oh they left, they didn't want any part of this," explained Ike.

"Boy you must be loco to give me a gun. Did you really think I was going to set up a dumbass son-bitch like you? Good-bye you dumb-ass clodhopper!" yelled

Harry. It only proved you're nothing but a lilly-livered coward with a gun," explained Ike. "Did you really believe I could sell out my family. Now you could with your little self-centered mind. Tell you what asshole, I am fixing to blow your knee-caps off. Now you can try to stop me anytime with a gun that has no firing-pin," stated Ike.

Harry jerked on the trigger. Ike intentioned slowly took out his gun fired.

An enormous amount of blood started to run down both legs. He fell screaming in severe pain on the hard ground. Laying beside the man, he wanted dead. "You two can enjoy each other company on your way to hell." Ike placed a bullet in each of the men's stomach.

Both men were gut-shot. They would suffer a long unbearable painful death. "Lay there and remember what you did to my wife and bovs on your journey to hell!" screamed Ike.

One of the remaining three men screamed, "quit dilly-dalling with us. have mercy on us."

Ike glared at the bulldozer of a man. "Did you have any mercy for me or my family?"

The big man pleaded, "don't kill me please. I don't want to die."

"Get out of my sight you coward. You make me sick to my stomach, you damn bastards." As Ike turned to walk away, he noticed three big buzzards flying low in the sky sensing the smell of blood. Ike walked toward his horse to leave two of the men figured Ike might change his mind later.

"Better get him now with his back to us. Someone yelled! "watch out!"

Spinning around he fanned his revolver, killing the two men. Feeling warm blood trickle down his back before he passed out.

When Cole and Sky-Hawk returned, a man was attending to Ike's wound. The bullet had torn into his right side missing bones and any organ. Only getting body fat.

An inch in the opposite direction, Ike probably be dead. If the young rancher, Johnny Fine had not warned him. He would have been dead. They had threated Johnny, saying something might happen to his family if he didn't take part in the killing of Ike's family. His only crime was he didn't try stop them.

Making him as guilty as they were. Lee Bannett let Johnny's small ranch join in the big ranches round-up. His sole purpose was to control Johnny. Plus, Lee had his eye on Johnny's beautiful wife.

They were returning home from a cattle drive celebrating their good fortunate. He got a very good price for the cattle. He paid off the men. Headed straight back without staying in town. Bannett told them, they needed to leave before the men got drunk and tore-up the place.

Everyone would expect them to pay all damages and fines. So they grabbed a couple bottles of whiskey and headed home. That's when they ran across Ike and his family.

Johnny's body began trembling as he relived that awful day. "I didn't have the courage to stop it. I deserve to be punished. I can't live with this guilt and shame."

Puzzled, Ike asked. "why did you warn me, all you had to do was let them kill me and it would be over."

"It will never be over for me. I'm tired of being a coward. I can't even look at my wife without thinking of that day. Please end it," begged Johnny.

"No I will not make it easy for you," Ike barked.

My advice to you is ask God, to forgive you, cause I cannot. Tell your wife what happen before someone else does. Maybe someday, you will find some peace with yourself," stated Ike.

Tears run down Johnny's face, "I pray someday you will forgive me."

"You need to go home, your wife is worrying about you," demanded Ike. He watched Johnny ride off, wishing that was him going home to his wife and boys. He noticed a chicken hawk circling looking for his prey.

His vendetta was finally over, but what now. He had no one except his two friends Cole and Sky-Hawk to lean on. A life-time friendship would develop among the three.

******

By 1875 President Grant replaced a corrupt judge with Judge Isaac Parker, 38 year old. His first order was to hire 200 deputy U.S. Marshals to bring law and order to Indian Territory. Some hired were black men because the Indians didn't trust white deputies. One was Bass Reeves, the first black deputy marshal west of the Mississippi.

Reeves who always rode a large white stallion, wore a large hat, wearing his two Colt pistols butt forward for a faster draw. Some other deputies were Rufus Cannon, Ike Rogers, Grant Johnson. A Choctaw lawman named Charles LeFlore. Also, in 1875, Sam Sixkiller was appointed High Sheriff of the Cherokee Nation and warden of the national prison at Tahlequah. Men you didn't want to mess with.

Ike thought serious about joining the elite group of men. But his friends, Cole and Sky-Hawk walked a thin line with the authorities. Ike didn't want to be put in a situation where he would be on the opposite side of them. So, he decided against it. Some people considered Cole a bad person 'cause he was a gunfighter, but he didn't choose that way of life. He just played the hand that life dealt him. Cole understood how Sam felt about losing a loved one to wicked men. He hated to see his son go down the same path that he went down. But a man is nothing without his honor. It was just a matter of time before someone begin bragging about killing Sam.

Finally, rumors started drifting back about a gunfighter and part-time gambler at Colbert Ferry. He was bragging about killing Sam and taking his guns as a souvenir. Sam's aunt fixed a huge breakfast that chilly morning. Few words were spoken. Sam led Midnight to Grace's grave to pray and pay his respects before heading out. His uncle, aunt and Ike watched him ride off into the morning sun.

Ike swore if anything happened to Sam, he would finish it for him. Sam had refused anyone to ride with him. Colbert Ferry was a crossing between Texas and Indian Territory on the Red River. The Chickasaw Nation had granted a fellow name of Ben Colbert permission to operate a ferry to cross the Red River. He charged twenty-five cents for man and horse. On the Texas side, about two hundred yards from the landing were some buildings. One building was named the 1st and Last Chance Saloon where whiskey was sold. In the back room, they played poker. Both the Texas road and the Butterfield mail route crossed into Indian Territory there. Colbert Ferry was an ideal spot for gamblers and crooks to wait for their prey to show-up. If a person wanted some whiskey, they better get it before entering Indian Territory where it was banned.

After three days of hard riding over some narrow trail, Sam arrived at Colbert Ferry. A sweating big burly man took him across with the wind blowing in their face. Stepping into Texas, Sam led Midnight to the stable where the owner was working at the forge rebuilding a wagon-wheel. Walking across the street, to the hotel. Sam noticed a flock of geese in the sky flying south. A short, nervous, older man sat behind the counter of the hotel. Sam got a room for the night. Stretching out on squealing bed, he soon was fast asleep. Sometime during the night, he was awakened by dogs barking. Next morning after a big breakfast, he walked over to the Last Chance Saloon.

He ordered a five cent shot of whiskey. Pushed a dollar bill over to the bartender with instructions to notify him at the hotel when a poker game started-up. A slim older bartender nodded his head in agreement. Sam hurried back to his room to lay down because he was getting a bad head-ache. Afraid he might have a blackout spell. Noise outside his room woke him.

Somebody hesitated, then knocked on his door. Pulling out his gun, but keep it hidden, he opened the door. A nervous red-head boy about twelve years old stood in the door way telling Sam the bartender sent him. Sam tossed the red-head, freckle-faced boy a quarter. He ran down the hall-way grinning yelling, "thank you mister."

Sam must have slept longer than he planned. Glancing out his room window, he saw it was late in the afternoon. He combed his hair after washing up. Putting on the guns his father gave him, he headed for the saloon. Entering the back room, he glanced around the smoke-filled room. It had a window on the south and east wall. Both windows needed cleaning. Curtains once white, looked a dingy yellow from all the smoke. Odors of cheap whiskey was present. In the center of room hanging from the ceiling was a huge lamp covering the poker table with six hard-wood chairs. A slim gray hair man, grizzled beard, wearing a Stetson hat with curved brim said, "sit if you want play. Name's Roy, own the hardware store next door. Sam pulled out some money and sat down. The man to Sam's left looked more like a drover and smelled like one. That left three men, he needed to watch. Not knowing what the killers looked like, he stayed alert. About two hours into the game, the drover questioned a hand being played.

The man sitting directly across from Sam became furious with the drover. He stood up grinning like a weasel in a hen house. "You calling me a cheat?"

The lanky redhead wore a fancy beaded buck-skin vest with shining buttons sporting a black bowler hat. Trying his best to goad the drover into a gunfight. A person could see he enjoyed killing. Sam noticed he was wearing his guns. The redhead told the drover, "a person ought to know who is going to kill him. The name is Chad Reed. I've killed twelve men and you're fixing to be thirteen."

"Take the pot Mister, I don't want any trouble, I'm no gunfighter," remarked the drover.

Jaws dropped and you could have heard a pin drop when Sam stood-up to face Reed. "Well if he's not calling you a card-cheating son of bitch. I sure am. You surely are the windies high-falutin bastard I have ever met. If you two men ain't with him, you better step over yonder. 'Cause today is Chad Reed's reckoning. The name is Sam Turley, you might say I have risen back from the dead."

Reed scorned with a half chuckle, "everybody knows I killed Sam Turley, got his guns to prove it, you're crazy as a loon."

"You and your family of bush-whackers dry-gulched me and my wife. You're lower than a snake's belly, you back-shooting bastard. I'm seeking justice for killing my wife," stated Sam.

Reed's face blushed pale white with terror, sweat dripped off his forehead. Knowing full well he was staring at death.

"Say howdy to the devil for me, 'cause you're sure'nuff gonna to see what hell looks like, you son of bitch!" shouted Sam.

Reed grabbed his drink, throwing it at same time and drew his shooting iron.

Sam's intentionally shot three of his gun hand fingers off before Reed's gun cleared the holster.

Sam wanted him to suffer and feel the pain for the emptiness he felt in his heart. Blood dripped onto the floor. Fingers lay on the floor soaked in bright red blood beside the gun.

"Pick-up the shootin' iron or tell me the names of the other men before I blow your damn head off!" screamed Sam.

Devastated, Reed glance, around the room seeking support. Howling, "you can't shoot a unharmed man in front all these witness or you'll hang."

"I don't see any witness, does anybody else?" asked Sam.

The room was completely silent, then the drover said, "I don't believe anybody heard or saw anything," giving Reed a faint smile.

Sam asked the older gentleman if he would mind writing down the names that Reed revealed to him. "Better be the right names, you sorry son of bitch or I'll be back to finish the job," demanded Sam. "I will stake you out on ant hill, pour honey all over your body, and watch the ants go to work on you. There'll be about a week of anguishing pain, then your body will swell up like toad-frog, your eye-balls will pop-out. You'll be begging to die. Now skedaddle back in your hole, you yellow-belly coward, before I change my mind. "I'll deal with you later."

Convinced he had all the names, Sam deliberately turned his back to Reed. To bait him to go for a gun. Hearing the clink of a gun, Sam whirled around putting a large cailber bullet right between Reed's eyes. The bullet exited the back of skull leaving a massive hole leaking out reddish-brown blood on the floor. Walking over to Reed life-less body, Sam reached down and retrieved his guns. The older gentleman handed Sam the list of names responsible for Grace's death. Sam walked out of the saloon toward the hotel. He noticed the marvelous sunset and remembered what his Cherokee grandmother always told him when they would watch the sunset.

"When the sun goes down, it always takes someone with it."

He wondered if it was revenge he sought or justice. Revenge was like a cancer, hard to rid yourself of it. Sam knew he could never rest until he saw that they all paid for Grace's death. Nothing else in this world mattered to him. He realized it was revenge that he sought. Sam devoted his life searching for the ones responsible. His reputation grew as Sam waged a personal vendetta against deadly odds.

The men on the list hired a hitman to kill Sam. A notorious gunman named Wade 'Snake' McBrian, a cold blooded professional assassin. Having keen black hollow eyes looking to strike down his next victim without warning. A thin man sporting a mustache, with black hair, and brush eye-brows. Wade usually killed his victim from a safe distance. He was a dead-shot with a gun, but his main desire was to have the reputation of a gunfighter, like Sam, not a back-shooter bounty hunter, Wade was a crazy lonely man who held-up in his hotel room for days drinking. He only trusted one woman, Mary, to enter his room to bring him whiskey. She sold information to him that she picked-up serving drinks. She was just about loco as Wade.

She was raunchy skinny with mouse brown hair. Her face looked like a dime's worth of dog meat. She looked so bad, her ears flopped. Mary brought Wade a bottle, with some big news to sell him if he was interested. It was about Sam Turley. Just hearing the name got Wade's immediate attention.

"You better tell me before I blow out what little bit of brain you have left.

Goosebumps broke-out on Mary's body 'cause she knew he would in a heartbeat. "Alright, the news is Turley's staying at Miller's house down by the depot. His friend, Bob Miller, is putting him on the first train heading north."

"Why would Turley get on train going North. It don't make any sense," answered Wade.

Mary nervously asked, "if I tell you, can I get my money?"

"Bitch, you better talk before I cut out your greedy slimy heart."

Her body trembled telling Wade that Sam had a bad seizure. His body functions were very weak and slow. They were putting him on the train to take him home for a complete rest.

The time was right for Wade to call Sam Turley out in the street for everyone to watch Sam get gunned down. After today, nobody would challenge him. He'd have the respect he desired as a gunfighter. Wade waited in the shadow of the alley close to the train station. A cat ran out of the alley shadows making Wade jump with fear. He's was nervous as a long-tailed cat in a room full of rocking chairs. He began to realize everything was happening too fast, he hadn't taken time to sort everything out. Maybe Sam wasn't that bad off. He knew Mary wouldn't cross him. She was that scared of him. Best thing was to wait and see how things played out.

Five minutes before the train was to pull out, Sam appeared escorted by two men holding him up.

Wade stepped out the shadows of the alley. Grinning like a possum eatin' a sweet tater. Knowing Sam wouldn't back down. No matter how bad off he was.

Wade shouted, "Turley, I'm calling you out. It's time you join your Indian slut. Alrighty folks watch Wade McBrian bring down the mighty Sam Turley!"

The two men with Sam stepped-aside.

Wade noticed Sam start to stand up straight. Wade begin to feel un-easy.

"Well little varmint, you want to be a big man.

Now your chance to ante up. You yellow-belly coward, you ain't gonna walk away from this. You call it now, make your play if you got the balls!" demanded Sam.

Wade hesitated trying to figure a way out. Realizing his back was up against the wall. He drew his shootin' iron. He was hit in chest almost as soon as he pulled his gun from the holster. Stumbling to the ground, Wade's eyes rolled back, fighting for air, looked up at Sam.

"Sorry pardner, but you called it, said Sam.

Coughing blood, Wade mumbled, you out foxed me. But I never believed Mary would sell me out."

Sam started to tell him she hadn't, but Wade took his last breath of air. Sam's friends had spread rumors around town, Sam was in bad way to out draw Wade out in the open. Sam actually had his seizures under control. As long as he smoked that wacky weed, the medicine man from his mother's tribe prescribe to him.

They begin hiring groups of men to hunt Sam down after that. His trusty trojan friend Ike rode by his side on a marvelous buckskin horse, telling Sam, he needed a little excitement in his life. He got plenty of action, the day they got drawn into an ambush by someone Sam had trusted. A group of men led by Colonel Ned Turner, a large man with a gray beard. He was wounded at Bitter Creek causing a bad limp The disability forced him out of the army making him a cruel and hateful man who drank too much.

They surrounded Sam and Ike at Clarksville on the Texas border. They fired into the old building until it was riddled with bullets. As it was getting close to dark, a thunder-storm blew in. Being tired and soak from the rain, the colonel made a critical mistake. Pulling everyone back to seek shelter and rest leaving four men to guard the building. The four men would be relieved every two hours until morning.

Seeing this, Sam and Ike waited for their chance. Everything depended on perfect timing, and a lot of luck. Ike told Sam to cover him. While he took care of the guards by slicing their throat. Surprising the two men quickly and slipping out of an almost certain death trap.

Riding hard north out of town into Indian Territory. Pushing their horses to put as much distance between them and the men as possible. The guards were not due to be relieved for another hour. Heavy rain help cover-up their tracks.

Sam and Ike needed a place to lay low to rest their horses and to come-up with a plan to rid themselves of the men chasing them. It was just a matter of time before they tangled with them again. One place they could stay and rest was an Indian camp. No white man would dare enter without being invited. Entering the Comanche camp, the dogs started barking, the children and squaws glared at the two strangers. Lot of braves were not in camp. Talking their language, Ike told them he spotted a small herd of buffalo a half day's ride to the southwest. Knowing they couldn't completely trust Ike. But they needed meat in a bad way. They agreed a couple braves would go with Ike, leaving Sam behind as a hostage if it was a trick.

A day later close to sunset, Ike and the braves returned pulling five buffalo on a make-shift sledge. Everyone who was able help in butchering and getting the meat ready. A brave informed them Sky-Hawk was attending a big pow-wow of all the Indian chiefs.

One brave offered to send word to Sky-Hawk letting him know of their presence. A few days later, Sky-Hawk arrived in the camp to the smell of buffalo meat cooking... The next day, Sky-Hawk sent out braves to scout the area. A few days later, around dusk, a scout returned to inform Sky-Hawk the men chasing Sam and Ike were camped twenty miles to the south and heading this way.

The next morning, Ike and Sam left the safety of the Indian camp. There was no need to put the women and children in danger. They turned their horses toward Elk Mountain, located in the Wichita Mountains, home to the Comanche, Kiowa and Apache tribes. In the distant foothills about a hard day's ride was Fort Sill, established in 1869.

Breaking the silence, Sam asked Ike, "how many you reckon are coming?"

"Oh, I would say enough to keep you busy for a spell. Ned and that bunch of bush-whackers got themselves duped. They got something to prove now. But just maybe, they will do something stupid," stated Ike.

Sam stared with admiration, "I'm sorry I got you in this mess."

Grinning, Ike said, "I wouldn't miss this for the world."

The next day around noon, Ned and his men were galloping toward them. With a stern voice Ike said, "wait, when we go, you stay close, got that?"

A couple minutes later, Ike barked, "let's get the hell out of here."

"Damn," Sam replied, "I was beginning to think you was hanging around to invite them to supper."

Keeping out of rifle range, they entered the mouth of a canyon. It was a box canyon with no way out except the way they had come in. Ned and his men rushed in thinking they had Sam and Ike trapped. Only to find Sky-Hawk and his braves along the walls of the canyon firing down on them. Losing ten of his men to a hail of bullets and arrows. Ned turned to retreat out of the canyon. Only to discover the mouth of canyon blocked. Nowhere to go.

Ned and his men were doomed to bite the dust. Sky-Hawk didn't try to stop the braves from rushing the remaining men. It was their battle and victory. Twenty-five bodies were scattered on the canyon floor. Braves danced with excitement scalping the bodies of the dead men.

"Dammit Ike, just when was you planning on telling me your plan?"

"Oh hell Sam," with a smile that illuminated his whole face. "Reckon I wanted to surprise you."

After the slaughter at Box Canyon, it became very difficult to get anyone to ride against Ike and Sam. Their reputation continued to grow. Sam's vendetta became what legends are made of.

Robert's voice brought Sam back to the present. "I was saying, we been at it a long time. Couple more questions and we'll retire for the night. When was you born Sam?"

"The year was 1848 in Indian Territory. My dad, Cole Turley was born in 1832. He received a medal at Gettysburg, fighting for the Union. His brother Luke and his brother in-law Lee fought for the Confederacy. "

Hesitating, Robert built up enough courage to ask a question about his father. "I hear your father was a gunfighter, also."

It took Sam a few minutes before he answered. "My father or I never sought to be gunfighters. Our journey in life took us down that path. It was our destiny to revenge our love ones."